Pirate Underpants!

D1421517

Published in 2012
by Wayland

Text copyright © Tom Easton
Illustration copyright © Matt Buckingham

Wayland
338 Euston Road
London NW1 3BH

Wayland Australia
Level 17/207 Kent Street
Sydney, NSW 2000

The rights of Tom Easton to be identified as the Author
and Matt Buckingham to be identified as the Illustrator of this Work have
been asserted by them in accordance with the Copyright, Designs and
Patents Act, 1988.

All rights reserved

Series Editor: Louise John
Editor: Katie Powell
Design: D.R.ink
Consultant: Shirley Bickler

A CIP catalogue record for this book is available from the British Library.

ISBN 9780750264921

Printed in China

First published in 2011, reprinted in 2012.
Wayland is a division of Hachette Children's Books,
an Hachette UK Company

www.hachette.co.uk

Pirate Underpants!

Written by Tom Easton
Illustrated by Matt Buckingham

WAYLAND

NEATH PORT TALBOT LIBRARIES	
2000640678	
PETERS	17-Feb-2016
JF	£4.99
Ske	

Captain Flint was in a bad mood. He called his crew up on deck. As they appeared bleary-eyed and half asleep, Captain Flint sighed miserably.

The trouble was his men didn't look much like pirates. Their clothes were ragged and they all looked tired and glum. Pegleg Pete's leg was full of woodworm and Long John's parrot had lost most of his feathers.

"It's been three weeks since we've captured any ships," the Captain bellowed. "You're a miserable excuse for a pirate crew. You're supposed to be stealing treasure and raiding other ships' food stores. You're just not trying hard enough."

"It's not us, Captain," said Selma. "We can't capture anything in this old ship. The Stuck Pig is too slow and her sails are falling apart."

"If only we had some decent sails, we'd
be the fastest pirates on the ocean!"
said Pegleg Pete.

"And the richest!" cried Arthur.

"What can we do, Captain?" asked Long John, miserably.

The pirates all looked up at the ship's sails. It was true. Each sail was full of holes and some sails were missing altogether! Captain Flint looked at his men, then back at the sails, then back at his men and smiled.

"I've had a **brilliant** idea!" he laughed.

The pirates spent all night working on the Captain's idea. The next morning, there were three new sails flapping in the breeze, patched up with the oddest and smelliest collection of pirate clothing ever seen on the Seven Seas.

"I can see my second-best pair of underpants," said Arthur, proudly, "right at the top."

"Now we'll catch those treasure ships!" the Captain boomed. "We'll steal their treasure and make the sailors walk the plank!"

"Arrr!" cried his men.

The Captain was right. The sails did work much better and it wasn't long before they saw their first ship on the horizon.

"What is it?" called Captain Flint to his lookout, Big Ben.

"Hard to see, Captain, but I think it's a Spanish ship. Full of Spanish silver, no doubt," Big Ben shouted back.

The Captain rubbed his meaty hands in glee.

The Stuck Pig slowly glided across the waves. The new sails were certainly better than the old holey ones but the pirate ship still wasn't the fastest on the Seven Seas!

"Hurry up!" cried the Captain in frustration.

At long last, the Stuck Pig drew level.
As the men were busy discussing how
to capture the ship, Selma grabbed
a rope and swung aboard the
Spanish ship.

"Come on, lads. Let's steal some silver!"
she shouted.

The other pirates looked at each other in shock and, not to be outdone, swiftly followed.

But the ship wasn't full of Spanish silver. It was full of Spanish soldiers, all dressed in bright blue jackets, while the Poor Pirates were scrambling about in their underpants. What a disaster!

19

Then something surprising happened.
One of the soldiers started giggling.
And then another. And another. Before
long the soldiers were in stitches at the
sight of six pirates in their underpants.

The Captain saw his opportunity.

"Quick lads," he whispered, "tie the soldiers up with this rope while they're distracted!"

His men didn't need to be told twice!
As quick as a flash, Pegleg Pete threw
the rope over the soldiers, bundling them
up tightly.

The others helped the Captain
to secure the men to the mast.

"We've captured the ship, Captain!"
cried Arthur happily, as he tightened
the rope's knot.

"Aye, but there's no treasure aboard,"
one soldier called out. "You've wasted
your time."

"I'm not so sure about that," said
Captain Flint. "You've got something
we really need."

"What's that, Captain?" asked Long John as he appeared from below deck, his arms full of food he'd stolen from the ship's galley.

The Captain pointed upwards. "Sailcloth," he said.

The pirates released the ship's sails as
the soldiers shouted angrily. They took
them, along with the ship's food stores,
back to the Stuck Pig.

"Wait! How will we get home?" cried
the soldiers, as the pirates set off.
"We have no sails."

"But you do have some lovely blue coats," called back Captain Flint. "If you sew those together, you'll have a fine sail!"

"Then you can travel back home in your underpants!" shouted Arthur Sandwich, and this time it was the Poor Pirates who roared with laughter.

The Poor Pirates worked all through the night once more and gathered on deck in the morning.

"Captain, would it not have been wise to use the sailcloth to make new sails instead of new clothes?" suggested Selma.

"No, Selma," Captain Flint chuckled. "We still may not be the fastest pirates on the Seven Seas, but now we're definitely the best-dressed!"

START READING is a series of highly enjoyable books for beginner readers. **The books have been carefully graded to match the Book Bands widely used in schools.** This enables readers to be sure they choose books that match their own reading ability.

Look out for the Band colour on the book in our Start Reading logo.

The Bands are:

Pink Band 1A & 1B

Red Band 2

Yellow Band 3

Blue Band 4

Green Band 5

Orange Band 6

Turquoise Band 7

Purple Band 8

Gold Band 9

START READING books can be read independently or shared with an adult. They promote the enjoyment of reading through satisfying stories, plays and non-fiction narratives, which are supported by fun illustrations and photographs.

Tom Easton lives in Surrey, works in London and spends a lot of time travelling between the two, which is when he does his writing. Tom has written books for children, teenagers and adults, under a variety of pseudonyms. He has three children and is looking forward to having macaroni cheese tonight.

Matt Buckingham would have rather liked a job as a pirate if he hadn't become an illustrator. The only problem is Matt gets seasick, so it's probably best if he sticks to drawing pirates instead.